BANGU THE FLYING FOX

BANGU THE FLYING FOX

A Dreamtime Story of the Yuin People of Wallaga Lake

We thank Mervyn Penrith who told his grandfather's story and gave permission for us to share it with you.

Story retold by Jillian Taylor

Illustrated by Penny Jones and Aaron Norris

ABORIGINAL STUDIES PRESS
CANBERRA 1994

This book is dedicated to Mervyn Penrith and our Dancers — Jo Angus, Celina Campbell, Stella Campbell, Emma Hankinson, Liza Morris, Serena Ridgeway, Melissa Walker, Alice Williams — and Mrs Pearson and Mrs Norris.

Author's note

Bangu the Flying Fox is a Dreamtime story told to us by the Umbarra Cultural Tour Group from Wallaga Lake, on the far south coast of New South Wales. This region has been the home of the Yuin people for many thousands of years. The Umbarra Cultural Tour Group are keeping the traditions of their people alive through their dedication and their work on the far south coast.

This story is retold with kind permission from Mervyn Penrith and the Umbarra Cultural Tour Group, by Jillian Taylor, and illustrated by Penny Jones and Aaron Norris. The authors, illustrators and Aboriginal Studies Press wish to record their thanks to Mervyn Penrith and the Umbarra Cultural Tour Group for their assistance.

First published in 1994 by
Aboriginal Studies Press for the Australian Institute of Aboriginal and Torres Strait Islander Studies, GPO Box 553, Canberra ACT 2601.

National Library of Australia Cataloguing-in-Publication Data:

Taylor, Jillian.
Bangu the flying fox.

ISBN 0 85575 257 2.

1. Flying foxes — Folklore. [2.] Aborigines, Australian — New South Wales — Wallaga Lake Region — Legends — Juvenile literature. I. Title.

398.245099447

4000 06 94

Produced By Aboriginal Studies Press
Typeset in Palatino, using Quark XPress
Printed in Australia by Griffin Press Limited, Adelaide

BANGU THE FLYING FOX

A Dreamtime Story of the Yuin People of Wallaga Lake

Long ago, when the world was new, there were many birds and . . .

There were many animals on the earth.

The birds and animals spent most of their time fighting one another. Bangu the Flying Fox couldn't make up her mind if she was a bird or an animal.

Bangu the Flying Fox liked to be on the winning side all the time. When she went out to play with the animals and they got into a fight with the birds, Bangu would change to the birds' side if they were winning.

If she was with the birds and the animals were winning, she'd change to the animals' side.

One day the birds and animals became really sick of this and had a big meeting. They were fed up with Bangu pretending to be one of them and changing sides.

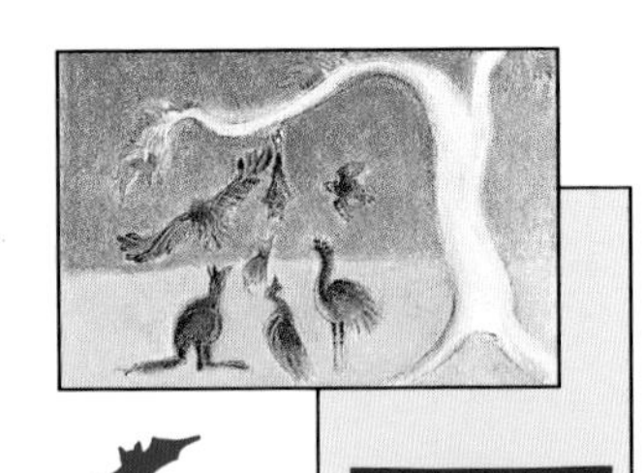

They called her over and told her off . . .
And,

Just to get the message across, they gave her a good hiding to go along with.

They said, 'Go away. You are not a bird, you are not an animal, and we don't want to play with you again.'

So Bangu crept away, and that's why you only see her come out at night and fly around by herself.

If you find friends, stick to them. Help them when things are good *and* when things are bad.

Because if you keep changing sides and letting your mob down, you'll end up as lonely as . . .

Bangu the Flying Fox.

Penny Jones has been working with the Koori children from Wallaga Lake for a number of years and has illustrated several children's story books.

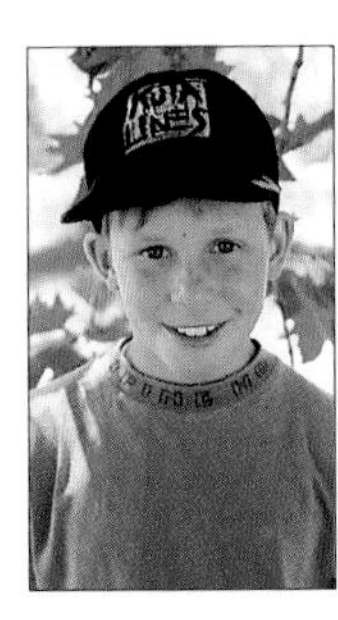

Aaron Norris is twelve years old and lives at Cobargo with his mum, dad and sisters, Yolanda and Tara. He enjoys karate, surfing, drawing and music.

Jillian Taylor is a teacher and lives near Wallaga Lake with her husband, Alan, and cat, Jovi, and has an enthusiastic interest in Aboriginal education and in literature and language.